FOUR STORIES

FOUR STORIES

❧

E T G A R   K E R E T

THE B. G. RUDOLPH LECTURES IN JUDAIC STUDIES

New Series, Lecture Six

Produced and distributed by Syracuse University Press
Syracuse, New York 13244-5290
All Rights Reserved

∞ The paper used in this publication meets the minimum requirements
of the American National Standard for Information Sciences—Permanence
of Paper for Printed Library Materials, ANSI Z39.48-1992.

For a listing of books published and distributed by Syracuse University Press,
visit our Web site at SyracuseUniversityPress.syr.edu.

ISBN: 978-0-8156-8156-4

Manufactured in the United States of America

CONTENTS

PREFACE

Ken Frieden

In October 2009, Etgar Keret visited Syracuse University and delivered the annual B. G. Rudolph Lecture in Judaic Studies. He spoke about his experiences as the child of survivors and read from his short fiction. Our publication of Keret's stories follows the precedent set by Aharon Appelfeld's "Badenheim 1939," which was published as volume 3 of the new series of B. G. Rudolph Lectures in Judaic Studies.

This sixth volume includes an edited transcript based on Etgar Keret's improvised comments and four of his short pieces. The first is a miniature called "Asthma Attack," which the author likes to call his *ars poetica*, a statement of his aesthetics. Each of the subsequent three stories—"Shoes," "Siren," and "A Foreign Language"—assumes the voice and perspective of a child of survivors.

Our intent is to give greater visibility to the cutting-edge fiction of Etgar Keret, whose writing is beginning to receive wide recognition in the United States. The success of his film *Meduzot* ("Jellyfish" or "Men of War"; 2007), directed with his wife, Shira Geffen, is a hint of many more honors to come. For devotees of Raymond Carver's minimalism and Robert Altman's *Short Cuts* (1993), Keret's writing is a revelation that points the way for many young Israelis. "We are all second generation," Etgar Keret told my students in a class at Syracuse University, echoing a line from the film *Meduzot*.

Much has changed in writing about the Holocaust in the past fifty years. Early chronicles in Yiddish and Hebrew were followed by Anne Frank's diary, Primo Levi's *If This Is a Man* (*Si questo è un uomo*), and Elie Wiesel's *Night* (*La Nuit*, adapted from his longer Yiddish version, . . . *Un di velt hot geshvign*). Since the 1960s, Aharon Appelfeld has called for more fiction about the Holocaust, to convey the depths of feeling beyond the historical details. David Grossman's *See Under: Love* (`*Ayen `erekh "ahava"*) compellingly presents the experiences of "Momik," an Israeli child of survivors. The parents' refusal to explain or discuss what happened "Over There" leads to imaginative displacements and distortions.

Etgar Keret's characters are rooted in the Israeli context, while at the same time their parents' pasts cast unpredictable shadows over their experience. Like Aharon Appelfeld and David Grossman, Keret tells these stories from a child's point of view. This lends them a distinctive charm, while hinting at ways in which the traumatic past continues to haunt the present.

In revising the transcript of Etgar Keret's Rudolph Lecture in Syracuse, we have retained the oral tone. Not only is colloquial speech a distinctive feature of his fiction; it embodies his way of approaching difficult subjects simply and without pretensions. Unadorned, Etgar's comments about his family, and his reflections on a second-generation childhood, are memorable and deeply moving.

INTRODUCING ETGAR KERET

George Saunders

My latest theory of fiction goes like this: rather than, say, a catalogue or a documentary account or a mirror-image of life, fiction is just a kind of big box. The reader enters the box. Inside there, something happens, and the reader emerges from the other side changed, in some nontrivial way. The change can be subtle and is always temporary, but like the changes caused by prayer or music, or a close call with death, the change is undeniable. And a series of such changes, absorbed over the course of a lifetime, can make that life more meaningful, and make the person who has absorbed those changes somehow more alive.

So when we talk about a writer, we're really talking about the particular flavor of inflection a trip through one of his boxes causes.

Which brings me to Etgar Keret.

When I go into one of Etgar's boxes, I come out—well, happier, for one thing. Energized. More aware. Kinder, somehow. I've had my heart tenderized and my honesty honed. I come out newly convinced that human beings, though doomed and inclined toward mischief, are still worth observing. His little boxes seem infused with the same qualities as Etgar himself: goodwill; a kind of joyful orneriness; a fondness for truth, even if that truth is of the discomfort-making variety; an essentially hopeful disposition toward God, mankind, and the world.

Etgar's stories are a reminder of that rude intangible that often goes unspoken in creative writing workshops: a great work of art is often just residual evidence of a great human soul. There is sweetheartedness and wisdom and eloquence and transcendence in his stories because these virtues exist in abundance in Etgar himself.

Reading his stories, we are reminded that what we call "craft" is really just the means by which the writer manages to give clear passage to these positive virtues.

Etgar's stories are often not strictly realistic, yet they are ultimately realistic. They say: Isn't this the way life really feels? Aren't these, in their essence, the problems we really face? And they go beyond this to do what is, in my opinion, the highest thing art can do: they offer comfort. They say: Well, yes, you are in a fix here, dear human, but you're not in it alone. I'm in that fix, too. Let's spend a few minutes pondering this fix we're in, with curiosity, with humor, with tenderness, and, in a way we don't quite understand, this mutual pondering will make things incrementally better.

I am very happy that Etgar and his work are in the world, making things better. I'm very proud to call him my friend, and to welcome him back to Syracuse tonight.

LECTURE

SECOND GENERATION

This is a very special evening for me, for many reasons. For one thing, it was worth traveling all the way to Syracuse to have a writer like George Saunders introduce me so warmly. But not only for that. Last year Ken Frieden suggested that I come to speak here, and we had a conversation; the idea came up that I would talk about myself as a second-generation writer. I said to Ken, "You know, actually I've been publishing for seventeen years and speaking about my writing for seventeen years, and I've never spoken about that. I think that could be nice."

Then before traveling to the United States, after I packed my suitcase, my wife looked at the suitcase and said, "Why are you taking along your wedding shirt? You never wear it." And I said to her, "You know, I have to speak in Syracuse, and I need a white shirt; and my wedding shirt is the only one I have." And she said, "But why do you need a white shirt to speak in Syracuse?" And I couldn't give a good reason. It had something to do with talking about being a second-generation writer. About my need to clarify to myself, even with this strange and completely internal dress code, that this isn't just another event for me.

The closer I got to this event, the more nervous I got—because I realize that being a writer demands from you some sort of sincerity and honesty. Basically, I think that you have to accept the fact that even the things that are objectively embarrassing are okay—when you put them out in the open and you're sincere about them. When people read my stories they learn something about me. That thing could be at times very

3

embarrassing, but by now I'm fine with it, and I'm fine with talking about those embarrassing things in public.

But I was never in a position where I was really talking about my family and especially talking about my family through this aspect—the fact that both my parents are Holocaust survivors. My mother is the sole survivor in her family from the Warsaw ghetto. She lost both her parents and her brother. My father, who lost his sister, survived with his parents by hiding in a hole in the ground for six hundred days. They had a local farmer feed them. After those six hundred days, when they pulled them out of that hole, none of them was able to walk because their muscles had stiffened.

In the early nineties, there was a trend. I'm sorry if I sound a little bit cynical, but in that period there was a huge, slightly shallow, public interest in the second Holocaust generation artist phenomenon. I myself had four offers by documentary filmmakers. They all wanted to make films about the fact that my parents survived the Holocaust and I turned out to be an artist. My impression was that the main reason the majority of those people approached me was not the nature of my work, but the simple fact that a bunch of these films which had just been made became very successful. Israeli musicians, Israeli authors, Israeli artists of all kinds, exposed their family stories and in that sense, they found a way of linking with the past and making the past relevant to their present. And I, for some reason, had a strong objection to that.

It's funny because around that time, they wanted to interview my mother for the Steven Spielberg archives, and she also refused to speak to them. And this is the way she said it: "I don't want people with cameras coming into my house and bringing mud into our living room." I remember her sharing this with me during a Shabbat dinner: "This woman was speaking to me. And all the time she said, 'But Steven Spielberg really wants to have *you* in the archive. But Steven Spielberg . . . '" And at some stage my mother said, "Why do you keep repeating his name? I didn't even like his movies!"

4

On another occasion, I think after my work was published in Poland—which is, ironically enough, the country where I'm most successful outside of Israel—she was offered an honorary citizenship by the president of Poland. Her reaction to that offer was that she said, "An honorary citizenship is something that you give some junkie rock musician. If you want to give me citizenship, give me a proper one." So my mom—she's a feisty one.

What I felt, I think, when they wanted to classify me under this second-generation token, was that it was some sort of a reduction of my family and of my relationship with my parents. It's as if they had found the words to say, "Okay. So this is *this* kind of family. And you are *this* kind of guy." And I refused that.

When you read second-generation authors, and there are some wonderful authors—children of Holocaust survivors, like Savyon Liebrecht, Lizzie Doron, Nava Semel, and now, recently, Amir Gutfreund—the thing that they always talk about is the silence. The fact that there was always a silence in their houses. Basically, Holocaust survivors did not talk about the Holocaust experience, either out of some wish to suppress the pain or even sometimes from a feeling of strong, unjustified, shame. They didn't want to tell those stories. I must say that in my house it was different, different in very strange ways that, as a kid, I was uncritical of—and I guess that also as an adult, I was uncritical. Maybe now after passing forty, I look at it differently, but my parents always had these things. You know, they never denied the horrifying experience they had to go through, but there was something in the way that they told it.

For example, my father spent almost six hundred days of the war in a hole in the ground, and I asked him, "Father, how did you get through that?" And he said, "You know, son, I have this belief that every person is the world champion in something. But the sad thing about it is, most of us will never discover what we are really good at. There are people who could be amazing tennis players, and they just play the piano all their life, and they are mediocre at that, and they don't know they could be great tennis players. One thing I can say about the war is that it showed me my greatest talent, the thing that nobody in the world can do better than me. And that's sleep! Throughout this long period, every day, I would close my eyes, fall asleep, wake up six or seven hours later, and I would say to my father, 'Dad, is the war over?' And he would say, 'No.' So I said, 'Maybe I should sleep some more.' This was my way of surviving the war. And all the people who were in hiding with me were jealous of me because they had to be there in a place in which time stood still, afraid for their lives, while I was sleeping."

I think that there is something in this story that tells about my connection to the Holocaust through my parents. I also suspect that the story is partly a lie, although my father does have a talent for sleeping as much as he wants. It's unbelievable, really. We had tough times in our family, and after he retired he went through cancer treatment. So at that time, he would say, "I want to sleep as much as I can." He would sleep twenty hours a day sometimes—it was unbelievable. And he is well.

So I'm sure that he lied, but there was something about the way that my parents were able to take those horrible materials and put them in some sort of frame that was almost optimistic. Once, I remember, I asked my mother, "How come, after you've seen such horrors, you still believe in people, and you're so optimistic about life?" And she said, "You know, when I grew up as a little child, I was living in hell. But since then, everything has kept improving." She said, "I guess my basic standard of human behavior was so low that the idea that people can be kind to each other— not kill each other, not kill children just for their ethnicity—was a huge surprise. It was like saying, 'Ah! Okay, so things are actually better than I thought they were.'" They always seemed to have a way of putting some sort of strength into things, putting their difficult life experience and what they've gone through into context. To extract from it some sort of beautiful thing, too, that can be said about humanity.

There are many things in my upbringing, I think, that came from the fact that my parents were Holocaust survivors. One thing that affected me a lot as a writer was the fact that my parents, being children of war, basically never had a normal childhood, and my mother was orphaned at an early age. They always said that they didn't know how to raise children, because they said that you usually look at your own childhood, and if your parents did a good job, you imitate them. If they did a bad job, you do the opposite. But they felt that they had no point of reference. They were always tied to the war, to wartime memories. And the thing that was very strong was that their parents would tell them bedtime stories. Being in hiding they had no access to books, so they would make up those stories. And my parents grew up with the feeling that a truly responsible parent can't just read a story from the book. He has to make it up. He has to bring something of himself, and he has to invest himself in that story. All my childhood, my parents would tell me stories, and all my father's stories always took place in bars. The protagonists were always prostitutes and drunks—because, again, my father didn't grow up in normal circumstances, so many things that happened to him in his teenage years are not things that usually happen to teenagers. But he would tell me those stories when I was five years old, and I knew all those beautiful, magical stories. I didn't know what a prostitute was, I didn't know what a drunk was; but what I knew was that people were good and they had a magical power to overcome all the bad circumstances around them. Because all of those stories were beautiful fairy tales that were like commercials for life and its potential. So I think that there was always a tension between something horrible—something that is completely illegitimate—and some beautiful human spirit behind it that compensated for that.

I think that growing up with this kind of optimism for a long time made me unaware for many years that, in some sense, there was also a very stressful side of dealing with the fact my parents were Holocaust survivors. On a conscious level, I always felt that everything was okay. But I guess it wasn't, and I often think, when I look at my career choice—becoming a writer—I can't look at that out of context, without looking at my sister and brother. We are three in my family. My sister is an ultra-Orthodox Jew, and she has eleven children and four grandchildren. She's forty-seven, so I bet there will be more. My brother is a very extreme left-wing political activist and social activist. And me—I'm a writer. I think that together, all of us—maybe we're not a Jewish mother's dream, I mean, doctors—but all of us, we were all going through this legacy and going down the road that our parents wanted us to go. And the road that they wanted us to travel was one that they couldn't actually explain or articulate, but what was very clear for us as children was that our parents basically were busy all their lives surviving, both physically during the war and after the war, not having any formal education, not having any family to support them, suffering from health problems. They basically were busy finding clothes, finding food, finding shelter. And when we were growing up, they gave us whatever we needed. It was almost as if they both believed that life had a kind of transcendent potential that they couldn't touch or they couldn't fully connect to, but that we could. In fact, metaphorically, they took us all the way to this wall, and they knew that on the other side of the wall was something that transcended material existence. And they felt that they couldn't get there, but it was our job to get there. If they could just lift us up or give us an extra push, we'd be able to see what's on the other side. Social activism, religion, and art are three different ways to transcend your material existence. And it's all a road that we've been sent on by our parents.

But I must say that their constant willingness to sacrifice everything for us was, in hindsight, difficult. They really don't understand how stressful it was for me, as a child, to grow up with parents who really don't want anything for themselves. And whatever they want, their greatest wish is just to give things to you.

So the first story I want to read basically has nothing to do in a direct way with the Holocaust, but it has a lot to do with my family experience of being second-generation. My father claims that of all my stories—and I have written many stories about my parents—this is the one that is the most factually true. I know it sounds strange, but that's what my dad says. It's called, "Pride and Joy."[1] [Etgar Keret reads the story "Pride and Joy."]

I must say one other thing about these stories. When I prepared this talk and reading, I realized that these were stories that I never read—neither in Hebrew nor in English. So I'm apologizing for not giving such a good reading. When you give a reading, you pick up certain stories and say, "Oh, I like this story. I want to read it." And there are some stories that you like, but you never read them in public; and you don't ask yourself why. And I guess that some of them put you in a vulnerable position, so you prefer not to read them.

Another thing about this experience, growing up with my parents being Holocaust survivors, was the fact that the Holocaust is an important part of Israeli identity. It's something that is constantly being taught in schools, and we have Yom ha-Shoah and children go to Yad Vashem and other Holocaust museums. I always felt a little bit confused in those places because there is something very simple and clear about the memory of the Holocaust on a national level, and on the educational level. The Jews are, of course, presented as victims. There were the Germans, who were victimizers. All those stories basically keep the same tone of—I wouldn't even say horror. Because when you go and mention the number of six million, then the feeling that you have is a feeling of awe, you are petrified. It's not that you can really feel the pain of those six million. You just feel that there is something there that paralyzes you. And I remember that one of the sentences that they would always tell us in school was that if you were not there, you would never be able to understand it. And I think

---

1. "Pride and Joy," translated by Sondra Silverston, is included in Etgar Keret's collection *The Nimrod Flipout* (New York: Farrar, Straus and Giroux, 2006), 49-54.

that, for kids, when a teacher says to you, "I'm going to talk to you about something, but you're not going to understand," this is kind of like saying you're excused. So there was something about it, that we would go through the motions, but we understood that we couldn't really understand. The teacher told us so.

When I told that sentence to my father, he was very angry. And he said, "Of course you understand." He said, "There is not one emotion that I have that you don't share with me. What it means to be afraid or cold or hungry—maybe I felt it ten thousand times more than you'll ever do. But you can understand it, for sure. And it's your duty to try and understand it. You cannot be excused from that." I think that there was something about my parents' childhood stories that was very humanizing and very simple—maybe not so simple, but something that you could touch—and that at the same time also contained some sort of ambiguity. I remember that my father would always tell me a funny story that happened to him in the ghetto. But he would also say that in Israel he could never tell the story because whenever he said, "I have this funny story that happened in the ghetto," people would ask him, "What ghetto?" He would tell them, and they'd say, "Did you lose any members of your family?" And he would say, "Yeah, I lost my sister." And they'd say, "How did you survive?" He'd say, "I was in a hole in the ground for six hundred days." By the time they said to him, "What was the funny story?" he didn't feel like telling it anyway. So there was something about him, that he almost felt cheated of the ability to share with other people things about his childhood and his young life. He said, "Those years of the war were the worst years of my life, but still, they were the years in which, for the first time, I kissed a girl, I smoked a cigarette, I grew up. They were my life." In a way, he wanted to fight to keep them that way.

When I grew up it was still, I think, near the end of the time when German products were boycotted by many Israelis, and Israelis refused to visit Germany. And my parents not only visited Germany, one of them had a very good friend who was German—and he wasn't only a German, but he was a soldier in the German army in the Second World War. He was older than my father. He fought with Rommel in Africa. He wasn't in the SS, but he was a German soldier. As a kid, I couldn't understand why there were all those things that everybody I knew respected, and my parents didn't. Didn't they know that the Holocaust was a horrible thing? Didn't they know that they're not supposed to speak to Germans? But they were able to carry some sort of ambiguity or complexity, which Sabras—native-born Israelis, who didn't have anything to do with the war—never carried because, for us, it was very simple. The Germans were bad. We didn't want to communicate with them in any way.

I think that the tension between those two kinds of memories appears in quite a few of my stories. I want to read one of them, which is called "Shoes." And it's also a story from child's perspective. [Etgar Keret reads the story "Shoes."]

Even if this wasn't conscious when I wrote it, I was trying to write about two kinds of memory: the memory of those kinds of mausoleums where you're supposed to be quiet and not touch anything; and the memory of the shoes that touches you all the time, and you get dirty, and you sometimes forget, but it's part of you. For me, the shoes are basically my parents and the memory of the Holocaust as I experience it through them.

Outside of Israel, the place where I'm most successful is Poland. The second place I'm successful in Europe is Germany. Poland and Germany are, of course, two countries that are very important, very relevant to my parents' past. When my mother had her seventieth birthday, I was a visiting professor in a German University in Berlin, the Free University. As a seventieth birthday present I invited her to Berlin for a few days, and the night she arrived I had a reading. We went to the venue, and as they always do, they put all of my books in the window of the bookstore. It was a very crowded reading. There were a lot of people, and afterward they bought books. I took my mother out for dinner, and we drank wine. She got a little drunk, and she talked to me. And she said that at some stage during the war, after her mother and brother died, she reached a breaking point. She couldn't take it anymore. She said to her father, "I don't care if the Germans kill me. I can't keep on fighting. I can't keep on going." And her father said to her, "But you have to stay alive because you have to take our family's revenge." My mother said that as a child she was very surprised, because it was a word that my grandfather had never uttered before in his life. And she said to him, "What do you mean? What am I supposed to do?" And he said, "What the Germans are trying to do is to wipe our name off this earth. And your revenge will be that you stay alive, and you will not let our name disappear. Tonight, after seeing you reading in this crowded bookstore," she said, "I feel I kept my promise to my father."

Edited by Ken Frieden

STORIES

ASTHMA ATTACK

When you're having an asthma attack, you can't breathe. When you can't breathe, you can hardly talk. Your sentence is limited to the amount of air you can get out of your lungs. Which isn't much. Three to six words maybe. Makes you realize how much a word is worth. You sift through the heaps of words that pop into your head. Choose the most important ones. And those cost you too. It's not like healthy people who throw out all the words waiting inside their head, like you throw out the garbage. When someone having an attack says *I love you* or *I love you madly*, there's a difference. A difference of a word. A word is a lot, because a word could be *stop*, or *inhaler*, or even *ambulance*.

Translated by Miriam Shlesinger

SHOES

On Holocaust Memorial Day, our teacher, Sarah, took us on the number 57 bus to the Volhynia Memorial Museum and I felt really important. All the kids in my class had families that came from Iraq, except me and my cousin and one other kid, Druckman, and I was the only one whose grandfather died in the Holocaust. The Volhynia Memorial Museum was a really fancy building, all covered in expensive-looking black marble. It had a lot of sad pictures in black and white and lists of people and countries and victims. We paired up and walked along the wall, from one picture to the next, and the teacher said not to touch, but I did. I touched one of them, a cardboard photograph of a pale and skinny man who was crying and holding a sandwich. The tears running down his cheeks were like the stripes that are painted down the middle of a street, and Orit Salem, the girl I was paired up with, said she'd tell the teacher on me. I said that as far as I was concerned, she could tell everyone, even the principal, I didn't care. That's my grandfather, and I'll touch whatever I want.

After the pictures, they took us into a big hall and showed us a movie about little kids being loaded onto a truck. They all choked on gas in the end. After that this skinny old guy climbed up onto the stage and told us how the Nazis were scum and murderers and how he got back at them and even strangled a soldier to death with his bare hands.

Djerbi, who was sitting next to me, said the old man was lying, and from the looks of him, there wasn't a soldier in the world he could beat up.

17

But I stared into the old man's eyes and I believed him. There was so much anger in them that all the attacks of all the hot-shot punks in the world seemed like small change by comparison.

In the end, after he was finished telling us about what he'd done in the Holocaust, the old man said that everything we'd heard was important, not just for the past but also for what was happening now. Because the Germans were still alive, and they still had a country. The old man said he'd never forgive them and he hoped we wouldn't either, and that we should never ever go visit their country, God forbid. Because when he and his parents had arrived in Germany fifty years ago everything looked really nice and it ended in hell. People have a short memory sometimes, he said, especially for bad things. They prefer to forget. But don't you forget. Every time you see a German, remember what I told you. And every time you see anything that was made in Germany, even if it's a TV—because most of the companies that make TVs, or anything else, are in Germany—always remember that the picture tube and other parts underneath the pretty wrapping were made out of the bones and skin and flesh of dead Jews.

On our way out, Djerbi said again that if that old man had strangled so much as a cucumber, he'd eat his T-shirt. And I thought it was lucky our fridge was made in Israel, because who needs trouble.

Two weeks later, my parents came back from abroad and brought me a pair of sneakers. My older brother had told my mother that's what he wanted, and she bought the best ones. Mom smiled when she handed them to me. She was sure I didn't know what was in the bag. But I could tell right away by the Adidas logo. I took the shoebox out of the bag and said thank you. The box was rectangular, like a coffin. And inside it lay two white shoes with three blue stripes on them, and on the side it said Adidas Rom. I didn't have to open the box to know that. "Let's try them on," Mom said, pulling the paper out. "To see if they fit." She was smiling the whole time—she didn't realize what was happening.

"They're from Germany, you know," I told her and squeezed her hand hard.

"Of course I know," Mom smiled. "Adidas is the best kind in the world."

"Grandpa was from Germany too," I tried hinting.

"Grandpa was from Poland," Mom corrected me. She looked sad for a second, but it passed right away, and she put one of the shoes on my foot and started lacing it up. I didn't say anything. I knew by then it was no use. Mom didn't have a clue. She had never been to the Volhynia Memorial Museum. Nobody had ever explained it to her. And for her, shoes were just shoes and Germany was really Poland. So I let her put them on my feet and I didn't say anything. There was no point telling her. It would just make her sadder.

After I said thank you one more time and gave her a kiss on the cheek, I said I was going out to play. "Watch it, eh?" Dad kidded from his armchair in the living room. "Don't you go wearing down the soles in a single afternoon." I took another look at the pale leather shoes on my feet and thought back about all the things the old man who'd strangled a soldier said we should remember. I touched the Adidas stripes again and remembered my grandpa in the cardboard photograph. "Are the shoes comfortable?" Mom asked. "Of course they're comfortable," my brother answered instead of me. "Those sneakers aren't just some cheap local brand, they're exactly the same ones that Pelé used to wear." I tiptoed slowly toward the door, trying to put as little weight on them as possible. I kept walking that way toward the petting zoo. Outside, the kids from Borochov Elementary School were forming three groups: Holland, Argentina, and Brazil. The Holland group was one player short so they agreed to let me join, even though they usually never took anyone who didn't go to Borochov.

When the game started, I still remembered to be careful not to kick with the tip, so I wouldn't hurt Grandpa, but as it continued, I forgot, just like the old man at the Volhynia Memorial Museum said people do, and I even scored the tiebreaker with a volley kick. After the game was over I remembered and looked down at them. They were so comfortable all of a sudden, and springier too, much more than they'd seemed when they were still in the box. "What a volley that was, eh?" I reminded Grandpa on our way home. "The goalie didn't know what hit him." Grandpa didn't say a thing, but from the lilt in my step I could tell he was happy too.

Translated by Miriam Shlesinger

SIREN

On Holocaust Memorial Day all the classes were taken to the school hall. A makeshift stage had been put up, and on the wall behind it they had stuck sheets of black construction paper with the names of concentration camps and pictures of barbed-wire fences. As we filed in, Sivan asked me to save her a seat, so I grabbed two. She sat down next to me and it was a little crowded on the bench. I put my elbow on my knee, and the back of my hand brushed her jeans. It was thin and nice to the touch, and I felt as if I was touching her body.

"Where's Sharon?" I asked. "I haven't seen him today." My voice was a little shaky.

"He's doing the naval commando tests," replied Sivan proudly. "He's already passed almost all the stages, he just has another interview to do."

At the other side of the hall I saw Gilead coming toward us down the aisle. "Did you hear that he's going to get the outstanding student award at the end-of-year party?" Sivan went on. "The principal has already announced it."

"Sivan," called Gilead as he came up to us, "what are you doing here? These benches are uncomfortable. Come on, I saved a seat for you in the back."

"Okay," said Sivan, giving me an apologetic smile and getting up. "It's really crowded here."

She went to sit with Gilead in the back. Gilead was Sharon's best friend, they played together on the school basketball team. I looked at the stage and breathed deeply, my hand still sweating. Some of the ninth graders got up on the stage and the ceremony began.

When all the students had recited the usual texts, an oldish man in a maroon sweater climbed onto the stage and told us about Auschwitz. He was the father of one of the students. He didn't speak for long, just fifteen minutes or so. Afterward we went back to our classrooms. As we went outside I saw Sholem, our janitor, sitting on the steps by the nurse's room, crying.

"Hey, Sholem, what's wrong?" I asked.

"That man in the hall," he said, "I know him. I was also in the *Sonderkommando.*"

"You were in the commandos? When?" I asked. I couldn't picture our skinny old Sholem in any kind of commando unit, but you never know.

Sholem wiped his eyes with the back of his hand and stood up. "Never mind," he said. "Go, go back to class. It doesn't matter."

I went down to the shopping center in the afternoon. At the falafel stand I met Aviv and Tsuri. "You heard?" said Tsuri, with his mouth full of falafel. "Sharon passed the interview today, then he'll have one little orientation course and he's in the naval commandos. You know what that means? They're hand-picked . . ."

Aviv began cursing—his pita split open, and the tehina and salad juice were dripping all over his hands. "We just met him on the basketball court. Gilead and him were celebrating, with beer and everything."

Tsuri giggled and choked and bits of tomato and pita flew out of his mouth. "You should have seen them joy-riding on Sholem's bike, like little kids. Sharon was thrilled to pieces he'd passed the interview. My brother said it's at the interview that most guys get thrown out."

I walked over to the school but no one was there. Sholem's bike, the one that was always chained to the railing by the nurse's room, was gone. On the steps there was a broken chain and a lock. When I got to school the next morning the bike still wasn't there. I waited for everyone to go to class and then I went to tell the principal. He told me I'd done the right thing, that no one would know about our talk, and asked the secretary to give me a late pass. Nothing happened that day or the day after, but on Thursday the principal came into our classroom with a uniformed cop and asked Sharon and Gilead to step outside.

The police didn't do anything to them, just gave them a warning. They couldn't give back the bike because they'd just dumped it somewhere, but Sharon's father made a special trip to school and brought Sholem a new mountain bike. At first, Sholem didn't want to accept it. "Walking is healthier," he said to Sharon's dad. But Sharon's dad insisted and in the end Sholem took the bike. It was funny seeing Sholem riding a mountain bike, and I knew that the principal had been right and I'd done the right thing. No one suspected that I'd told on them, at least that's what I thought at the time. The next two days passed as usual, but on Monday when I came to school, Sivan was waiting for me in the yard. "Listen, Eli," she said, "Sharon found out it was you who told them about the bike; you've got to get out of here before he and Gilead get hold of you."

I tried to hide my fear, I didn't want Sivan to see it.

"Quick, run away," she said.

I started to walk away.

"No, not through there," she said, pulling my arm. The touch of her hand was cool and pleasant. "They'll come through the gate, so you'd better go through the hole in the fence behind the sheds."

I was glad that Sivan cared so much for me, even more than I was scared.

Sharon was waiting for me behind the sheds. "Don't even think about it," he said, "you haven't got a chance."

23

I turned around. Gilead was standing behind me.

"I always knew you were a worm," said Sharon, "but I never thought you were a rat."

"Why did you tell on us, you piece of shit?" said Gilead, giving me a hard shove. I stumbled into Sharon and he pushed me away.

"I'll tell you why he ratted on us," said Sharon, "because our Eli is jealous as hell. He looks at me and sees that I'm a better student, a better athlete, and I've got a girlfriend who's the prettiest girl in the school, while he's still a poor virgin and it eats him up."

Sharon took off his leather jacket and handed it to Gilead. "Okay, Eli, you did it, you screwed me," he said, taking off his diver's watch and putting it into his pocket. "My dad thinks I'm a thief, the police almost charged me. I won't get the outstanding student award. Are you happy now?"

I wanted to tell him it wasn't that, it was because of Sholem who was also in a commando unit, because he cried like a baby on Holocaust Memorial Day. Instead I said, "It's not that at all . . . you shouldn't have stolen his bike, it didn't make sense. You have no honor." My voice shook as I spoke.

"You hear that, Gilead, this whining rat is telling us about honor. Honor is not telling on your friends, you shit," he said, balling his fist. "Now Gilead and me are gonna teach you all about honor the hard way."

I wanted to get away from there, to run, raise my hands to protect my face, but fear paralyzed me. Then suddenly, out of nowhere came the sound of the siren. I'd completely forgotten that it was Memorial Day for the Fallen Soldiers. Sharon and Gilead came to attention. I looked at them standing there like shop window dolls and suddenly all my fear went away. Gilead, standing rigidly to attention, eyes closed, holding Sharon's jacket, looked like an oversized coat hanger. And Sharon, with his murderous look and clenched fists suddenly looked like a small boy imitating a pose he'd seen in an action movie. I walked to the hole in the fence and stepped through slowly and quietly, while behind me I heard Sharon hiss,

"We're still going to fuck you." But he didn't budge. I went on walking home through the streets with all the frozen people looking like wax dummies, the sound of the siren surrounding me with an invisible shield.

Translated by Anthony Berris

A FOREIGN LANGUAGE

For his fifty-first birthday we bought Dad a pipe. Dad said thanks, ate a piece of the cake that Mom had baked, and kissed everyone. Then he went into the bathroom to shave. He was one of those fanatical shavers who go over each section three times and emerge perfectly smooth, without a nick. In my entire life I've never seen Dad nick himself even once.

Some people know French or Italian, all kinds of languages. Which they studied by correspondence or in courses run by the consulate. Take my older brother, he studied German once at the Goethe Institute. You never know when a foreign language might come in handy. Not only on trips abroad; sometimes it could actually save your life. My mother in the Holocaust and the German language, for instance, is a good example.

Once my father had finished going over each section of his face three times, he started on the back of his neck. The razor wasn't built for that, and he had to spend half the time pulling out the thick hairs that got in the way of the blades. It was a hard and thankless task, and he was dying to call me into the bathroom to tell me about it. He wanted to tell me something about how if he hadn't married my mother he would definitely have gone to Scandinavia and built himself a cabin in some godforsaken forest and sat on his balcony every evening, smoking his pipe.

My girlfriend once asked me to tell her I loved her in a different language, an exotic one. And no matter how hard I tried and tried and thought and thought I just couldn't think of a thing. "Hebrew isn't good enough? Or Pig Latin?" I tried, "Atin-lay ig-pay? What if I say it twice? If

27

I really and truly mean it?" It wasn't good enough. She didn't calm down, and she just went on and on screaming—she can be that way sometimes. In the end she threw a heavy ashtray at my head, one with an insurance company logo, and I had blood running down my forehead. "Love me, love me," she yelled. And I tried as hard as I could to think back over the things that the Russian guys at work had taught me, but all that came into my head were curses.

Dad went over the back of his neck five times. When he was through and ran his hand over it, it was at least as smooth as his cheeks. The reason he wanted to build the cabin in a forest in Scandinavia was mainly because of the quiet. My dad really loved quiet. When my brother and I cried as children it bugged him so much that sometimes he just felt like strangling us. My dad took a can of special glue and a thin piece of wood like a popsicle stick from under the sink. He dipped the stick in the tin can and started spreading glue over the back of his neck. It was a complicated procedure, because he couldn't see the surface he was covering, which is like spreading butter over a slice of bread when it's facing down. But my father didn't lose his cool, and kept spreading the sections of the back of his head very patiently and with the utmost precision. While he was doing it, he hummed a Hungarian ditty that went more or less like this: "Ozo sep? Ozo sep? Okineki semmet lep. Okineki semet fakete."

"Who's the most handsome? Who's the most handsome? The one with the dark eyes. He's the most handsome." And after throwing the ashtray at my head she left me. To this day I have no idea why. But you don't always have to understand to learn from something. And to learn something important. My mother, for example, told the German officer not to kill her. She'd make it worth his while, because if he didn't kill her she'd sleep with him willingly. Which was far less common than rape in those days. And then, when they were doing it, she pulled a knife out of her belt and sliced open his chest, just like she used to open chicken breasts to stuff with rice for the Sabbath meal.

My father put the plug in the bathtub drain and turned on the water, not too hot and not too cold. Just right. Then he lay down in the bathtub holding his neck up above the water, and reached for the faucets, like so, lying on his back. The faucets were too high. My father relaxed his neck muscles and let the back of his neck stick to the bottom of the bathtub. He did everything he could to lift up his head but he couldn't. The flier that came with the glue promised that no amount of water in the world would succeed in removing it. As for the plug—he was wearing shoes. Let's see you pull a plug when you're wearing shoes. Meanwhile, in my room, my brother and I were having an argument. I said Dad really liked his present, my brother said he didn't. We couldn't arrive at a clear conclusion, because with my father, you never know. *Bloop-bloop-bloop*, the water in the bathtub murmured in Scandinavian. "Nur Gott weiss," my brother said, showing off his German. "Only God knows."

Translated by Miriam Shlesinger

BIBLIOGRAPHICAL INFORMATION

Original places of publication for the stories included in this volume:

ENGLISH

"Asthma Attack," translated by Miriam Shlesinger, was published in Etgar Keret's
    The Girl on the Fridge (New York: Farrar, Straus and Giroux, 2008).
"Shoes," translated by Margaret Weinberger Rotman, was first published in Etgar
    Keret's *The Bus Driver Who Wanted to Be God & Other Stories* (New York: St.
    Martin's Press, 2001), and reprinted (London and New Milford, Conn.: The
    Toby Press, 2004).
"Shoes," translated by Miriam Shlesinger, was later published in *Missing Kissinger*
    (London: Chatto & Windus, 2007), and reprinted (London: Vintage, 2008).
    Our reprint of this story is based on Miriam Shlesinger's translation.
"Siren," translated by Anthony Berris, was published in Etgar Keret's *The Bus Driver
    Who Wanted to Be God & Other Stories* (New York: St Martin's Press, 2001), and
    reprinted (London and New Milford, Conn.: The Toby Press, 2004). Our reprint
    of this story has been edited by Ken Frieden in consultation with the author.
"A Foreign Language," translated by Miriam Shlesinger, was published in Etgar
    Keret's *Missing Kissinger* (London: Chatto & Windus, 2007), and reprinted
    (London: Vintage, 2008). This story has not previously been published in the
    United States.

HEBREW

"Asthma Attack" and "Siren" were first published in Etgar Keret's first story col-
    lection, *Tzinorot* [Pipelines] (Tel Aviv: 'Am 'oved, 1992).

"A Foreign Language" and "Shoes" were first published in Etgar Keret's second story collection, *Ga'agu'ai le-Kissinger* [Missing Kissinger] (Tel Aviv: Zmora-Bitan, 1994).

BIOGRAPHICAL NOTE

Born in Tel Aviv in 1967, Etgar Keret is one of Israel's most popular authors. His books have received international acclaim and have been published in twenty-eight languages. In English translation, Keret's writing has been published in distinguished venues such as *The New York Times*, *Le Monde*, *The Guardian*, and *The Paris Review*.

Goran Dukic's film *Wristcutters: A Love Story* (2006), based on Keret's short story "Kneller's Happy Campers," received attention because of its candid grappling with suicide. In 2007, Keret and Shira Gefen won the Cannes Film Festival's Camera d'Or Award for their movie *Jellyfish* (*Meduzot*). *The Meaning of Life for $9.99*, a stop-motion animated film co-written by Keret and based on his short stories, was released in 2009. Keret currently lectures in the Department of Hebrew Literature at Ben Gurion University.